Published by Sunbird Books, an imprint of Phoenix International Publications, Inc.

8501 West Higgins Road   59 Gloucester Place
Chicago, Illinois 60631   London W1U 8JJ

www.sunbirdkidsbooks.com

Text and illustrations © 2021 Sally Anne Garland

Library of Congress Control Number: 2020944606

ISBN: 978-1-5037-5866-7 Printed in China

The art for this book was created with pencil and paper and the aid of a computer.
Text set in Pinch.

Stuck INSIDE

Written and illustrated by Sally Anne Garland

sunbird books

Toby had hurt his little paw
and had to stay in from his
usual walks until it got better.

Tilly also had to stay inside,
until the big storm passed by.

Poor Toby. He paced back and forth at the front door...

...while Tilly gazed sadly out of the window at the dark, gathering clouds.

Then, the little dog brought something that belonged to the outside...

...and placed it hopefully
at Tilly's feet.

It was his leash, and it gave Tilly an idea of what they could do.

Together they began to explore the inside looking for all their outdoor belongings.

Nervously they opened doors that had always seemed closed and peered into darkened corners.

They inspected under
beds for hidden stuff
that might lie beneath...

...and peeked into spaces they had never before explored.

They scoured the tops of shelves and uncovered dusty things long forgotten.

Between them, they discovered
lots of interesting things.

Things they had not noticed...

...and toys they had not remembered.

Old walking sticks.
Umbrellas with
bent spokes.

Skateboards, roller skates, and lots
of different kinds of balls.

Bicycles, jump ropes...

...and even a big,
flattened wading pool.

Tilly and Toby gathered
all these things into a great,
big pile of outside stuff...

...and decided to make something good out of what they had.

As they moved and carried things,
they planned the games they
would soon play...

...and as they tweaked and twiddled things, they remembered places they had been and looked forward to seeing again.

Together they created fantastic
adventures in their imagination,
until they stood back and marveled
at what they had made...

...something truly wonderful, out of all the outdoor things they had found.

The most amazing, astounding, and spectacular Dog-Walking, Storm-Protecting Machine!

They played with it for ages and forgot that they were stuck indoors.

Nor did they realize in all their excitement that they had also discovered another wonderful thing.

That all the fun of outside...

...was already inside their minds.